Cid's Quest

by Michael Toro

for
Mom and Tommy

Acknowledgments

A wise man once stated that it is a terrible thing that, when we speak of those exalted and celebrated in accomplishment, we fail to mention the inner struggles and impediments that plagued them along the way. I can relate this saying to my mother and brother, since, being the youngest member of our small family, I was in a unique position to watch their own struggles and accomplishments. For me, their refusal to ever give up became a measuring stick, and their love became the root from which I grew as a young man.

I wish to thank my daughters, Stella and Ilana, for their unwavering love and affection. You girls certainly carry the same family seeds within you. To my wife, Heather: your actions embody the true meaning of the word *encouragement.* I love and thank you.

To my partner in crime, Andy Lacayo: thank you for your talents and friendship.

Michael "Wheaty" Toro

Early rise

A hazy, early morning fog hung over the small San Mateo peninsula town as a young boy awoke to the sounds of his alarm clock. Cid, twelve years young, had barely rubbed the sleep out of his eyes when he heard the loud thump at his front door under his room. Looking out of his window, he saw the newspaper delivery truck speeding off down Twenty-Sixth Avenue, leaving a bundled pile of today's early headlines stacked at the door.

He closed his curtain, turned to look at his closet door in front of his bed, and stared intently at a picture of a trophy he had cut out from the Sports section of The Peninsula Times and tacked to the door almost a year ago. He spent a few moments in deep thought, until the sound of a snoring six-year-old distracted him. Across the room was his little brother, Wheaty—an energetic boy who looked up to his brother the way moviegoers in the 1940s praised their matinee idols.

Cid tossed an extra blanket on little Wheaty and quickly changed into his delivery clothes, splashed some water on his face, and headed downstairs to fold and bag his newspaper deliveries for the day.

Cid both loved and dreaded his newspaper route. The morning cold was unkind while riding his Mongoose bicycle; the hills in the peninsula were enough to defeat even a grown man. But to Cid they were a needed challenge, for this was not only a time to work but also to train.

After last year's second-place finish in the seventh-grade one-hundred-meter championship, Cid trained tirelessly every morning for one year and rode his bicycle up the hills of his delivery route with the vigor of a Marine landing on the shores of Tripoli. The loss, along with his family's financial struggles, only added to the heavy burden that plagued Cid to accomplish something. Losing the race reminded him of how far he was from being a winner. So, he trained while he worked and thought of the trophy to remind him of the dream he intended to capture. For one year he rose from bed with a purpose. A focus. A hunger.

Cid returned from his route and as he entered through the front door, a familiar odor warmed his senses. He walked into the kitchen where his mother, Rachel, happily greeted him as she was preparing his Cream of Wheat and her usual percolated coffee from her favorite piece of blue-flowered Corning Ware.

Suddenly hearing a loud stomping sound, Rachel and Cid turned to each other and smiled as the mini hurricane, Wheaty, was sprinting down the stairs into the kitchen; he was anxious for some breakfast, as he launched himself like Walter Payton into his big brother's arms. A small family of three, they were.

Rachel, a dedicated mother, not only labored at work all day, but also spent her evenings attending classes at the local junior college to obtain her associate degree that would help her earn a job promotion.

To say times were hard on Rachel and the boys was an understatement. As much as Rachel worked furiously to make ends meet, she continually came up short. After several trips to the electric company to restore power to her house, she realized she could no longer afford the family home and reluctantly put it up for sale. A quick sale in a seller's market allowed Rachel to rent an apartment close by, only to have the buyer withdraw thirty days later, leaving her with both a high mortgage and new apartment lease to pay. The incident caused a financial whiplash that depleted her humble savings account.

The following months Rachel lived on borrowed money from her best friend Gabriella's parents. Gabriella had shared Rachel's struggles over dinner one evening with her parents. The story resonated with Gabriella's father, a former immigrant who had moved to the Bronx with his widowed mother and younger siblings some time ago. After dinner, Mr. Philippe handed Gabriella a check to give to Rachel on the condition that she not feel obligated to pay him back. Mr. Philippe believed that the true blessing was his, and that no amount of money could generate the gratification he felt in helping Rachel and the boys. He loved the idea of going back in time and slapping adversity in the face.

One afternoon, Gabriella and Rachel met at Heidi's Pies for lunch and freshly baked strawberry pie. After their hearty meal and fun filled conversation, Gabriella paid the waitress and handed Rachel an envelope containing her father's check. Gabriella, expecting Rachel to automatically reject the money, calmly said to her, "Think of the boys." And with that, Rachel took a moment and was suddenly overcome with emotions ranging from sensational relief to a strange frustration that someone, however kind, had to rescue her.

The wonderful gesture from Mr. Philippe not only helped defeat the financial onslaught that had depleted Rachel's savings account but also added fuel to the fire of this single mother to work relentlessly to slay her financial shortcomings that had overwhelmed her life and threatened her boys' futures. With the family home now finally sold, Rachel and the boys settled into their new affordable apartment just down the street from school. With the earnings from the sale, Rachel was able to pay for the rest of her classes at City College and complete her degree on time.

This earned her a promotion at work along with a nice pay raise. As a gesture of thanks, Rachel mailed a thank-you card and a copy of her degree to Mr. Philippe, along with a check with the words *Blessing received* written on the memo line.

Her efforts did not go unnoticed, as she was Cid's beacon and measuring stick for his internal greatness. For Cid, greatness was something felt, not bestowed by others. After all his failings in track and field, along with his academic attempts to get accepted to the prestigious Padre High School down the street, Cid was as focused and determined as ever to feed his internal seeds of greatness.

This weekend presented him the opportunity to win and feel whole again. The eighth-grade boys hundred-meter Peninsula Championship race was scheduled, and Cid was prepared more than ever to win.

He had gone head to head with his competition all season leading up to the championship games and maintained a calm fury as the season progressed. Coach Walsh always used Cid as his example of "H and H" (heart and hustle) to his team. Cid, always humble and a bit shy, would anxiously walk away from such praise.

The following day at school, Principal Aguirre held a pep rally the day before the race, marching all the track and field competitors from Gregory Elementary through the gymnasium and onto the stage for a proper send-off. This celebration left a bitter taste in Cid's mouth, as defeat usually followed such pageantry. While standing on stage in front of the student body, Cid promised himself he would leave it all on the track, win or lose, at tomorrow's race.

The Race

A sunny morning greeted Rachel and Wheaty, as they waited outside for Cid in Rachel's '79 Ford Granada. In his bedroom Cid looked at the picture of the trophy one last time, as he grabbed his track shoes and headed down to the car. The image of the trophy was now ingrained in his mind.

At the track Rachel and Wheaty anxiously walked up to their seats in the metal bleachers, while Cid stretched on the football field that was still moist from the morning dew. An official alerted the runners to get to their lanes. Cid lined up in lane four, as the other competitors stepped into their ready positions. Cid positioned himself in his lane. Lean and fit with a freshly shaved head, he was hungry for victory. He had put his heart and mind into becoming a great runner, only to be met by defeat time and time again.

But this time—this time Cid was committed to the task at hand. As the race official announced to the runners to get set, Rachel, with her eyes filled with tears, looked out at her young and determined boy with a sense of pride. Wheaty, ever energetic, decided to stand and watch his hero. Cid stared down his lane, his eyes piercing, his breath calm and deep, his heartbeat ratcheting up—and his eyes on the prize.

The starting gun fired, and in that moment released Cid into a fierce sprint down the lane, pumping his arms and heating the soles of his shoes on the rubber track. Cid's eyes welled with tears, and his focus grew even more intense, as he approached the finish line.

Across the line like a comet, Cid let out a scream, releasing the inner demon that had lived in him for the past year. Victory was Cid's this day, an uncommon result for a kid like Cid. Inspired and excited, Cid headed for the parking lot. He had won. He felt no desire to attend the awards ceremony, as the trophy had already resided in his heart. No amount of tin and wood could replace something as valuable as what was now inside of him: character. Learning he had character was his true reward today.

Rachel's celebration turned to an anxious moment, as she observed Cid's actions; she let out a loud gasp as she ran from the stands in a hurry, stumbling over seated spectators along the way. Running anxiously down the track, she grabbed Cid, before he made his extraordinary exit for the parking lot. She pulled him close to her and embraced him while smiling wide and cradling his sweaty head against her chest, proud today of her boy's accomplishment.

Wheaty was still in the bleachers and jumping up and down like a circus chimpanzee, oblivious to his surroundings while overcome with joy. Rachel calmly turned Cid around, and together they headed back toward the track. The officials, all with curious looks on their faces, waited patiently for today's peculiar champion.

Cid